W9-BKL-540

The Cam Jansen Series

Cam Jansen

and the
Secret Service
Mystery

David A. Adler

illustrated by
Susanna Natti

VIKING

James Russell Lowell

30051000000271

Published by Penguin Group
Penguin Young Readers Group, 345 Hudson Street,
New York, New York 10014, U.S.A.
Penguin Group (Canada), 90 Eglinton Avenue East, Suite 700, Toronto,
Ontario, Canada M4P 2Y3 (a division of Pearson Penguin Canada Inc.)
Penguin Books Ltd, 80 Strand, London WC2R 0RL, England
Penguin Ireland, 25 St Stephen's Green, Dublin 2, Ireland
(a division of Penguin Books Ltd)
Penguin Group (Australia), 250 Camberwell Road, Camberwell,
Victoria 3124, Australia (a division of Pearson Australia Group Pty Ltd)
Penguin Books India Pvt Ltd, 11 Community Centre, Panchsheel Park,
New Delhi - 110 017, India
Penguin Group (NZ), Cnr Airborne and Rosedale Roads, Albany,
Auckland 1310, New Zealand (a division of Pearson New Zealand Ltd)
Penguin Books (South Africa) (Pty) Ltd, 24 Sturdee Avenue, Rosebank,
Johannesburg 2196, South Africa

Penguin Books Ltd, Registered Offices: 80 Strand, London WC2R 0RL, England

First published in 2006 by Viking,
a division of Penguin Young Readers Group

1 3 5 7 9 10 8 6 4 2

Text copyright © David Adler, 2006
Illustrations copyright © Susanna Natti, 2006
All rights reserved

LIBRARY OF CONGRESS CATALOGING-IN-PUBLICATION DATA
Adler, David A.
Cam Jansen and the secret service mystery / by David A. Adler ;
illustrated by Susanna Natti.
p. cm. – (The Cam Jansen series ; 26)
Summary: Cam and her friend Danny help solve the mystery of
a stolen pearl necklace when the governor comes to visit their
school for the dedication of the new library.
ISBN 0-670-06092-5 (hardcover)
[1. Schools—Fiction. 2. Governors—Fiction. 3. Mystery and detective stories.]
I. Natti, Susanna, ill. II. Title.
PZ7.A2615Caqkh 2006
[Fic]—dc22
2005033490

Manufactured in China
Set in New Baskerville

For Michael, Deborah, and Jacob
—D.A.

To my mother,
Lee Kingman, with love
—S.N.

CHAPTER ONE

"Please, please, don't put me in jail!" Danny called out.

The other children in the classroom turned and looked at Danny.

"Who's putting you in jail?" Cam Jansen asked.

Danny stood by his desk. He spread out his arms and shouted, "I tell you, I didn't do it!"

"What didn't you do?" Eric Shelton wanted to know.

"They've come to get me! This is terrible! They've come to get me!"

"What are you shouting about?" their teacher, Ms. Benson, asked. "What didn't you do? Who has come to get you?"

Danny pointed out the window.

Four police motorcycles, two long black cars, and a news truck had stopped by the front of the school.

"It's the governor and the Pearls," Ms. Benson said. "They haven't come to arrest anyone. They've come to dedicate the school's new library."

Danny fell back on his chair. He looked up at the ceiling and sighed. "I thought I was a goner."

The other children in Ms. Benson's class rushed to the windows. They watched as the police officers got off their motorcycles and opened the door of the first black car. Two men and two women, each wearing a black jacket and black pants, and each holding a walkie-talkie, got out.

"They're Secret Service agents," Ms. Benson said.

The two men were tall. One was bald. The other had short dark hair and a mustache. The women were tall, too. One had long blonde hair. The other woman had dark hair.

The agents looked around.

The blonde woman tapped her hand on the roof of the car, and a man in a blue suit

got out. He smiled at the police officers and the people dressed in black.

"That's Governor Zellner," Ms. Benson said.

The governor went to the second car. He opened the back door, and an elderly couple got out.

"Those are the Pearls," Ms. Benson told the class.

Eric looked at his watch and said, "They're early. It's only nine forty and the program starts at eleven."

"I don't think so," Cam said. She closed her eyes and said, "*Click!*

"The program starts in the new library at ten," she said with her eyes still closed. "The fourth- and fifth-grade classes will be there. At eleven Governor Zellner will visit the first, second, and third grades. Then he'll read stories to the children in kindergarten."

The program was posted on a large sign in the front hall. Cam had seen it when she came to school. Now, with her eyes closed, she was looking at a mental picture she had of the sign.

Cam Jansen has what people call a photographic memory. It's as if she has pictures in her head of whatever she sees. When she wants to remember something, she closes her eyes and says, *"Click!"* She says it's the sound her mental camera makes.

Cam's real name is Jennifer, but when people found out about her amazing memory, they called her "The Camera." Soon "The Camera" became just "Cam."

"Please," Ms. Benson said, "return to your seats."

When the children were seated, Ms. Benson told them, "It's a great honor for us to meet the governor." Then she looked at Danny and said, "I expect everyone to be on his best behavior."

"Hey! What did I do?" Danny asked.

"I'm serious," Ms. Benson told him.

Beth raised her hand and asked, "Why did the Secret Service people come here?"

"They've traveled with Governor Zellner ever since he said he was running for president."

"Of the United States?" Danny asked.

"Yes," Ms. Benson answered.

"Wow!" Eric said. "I might meet the next president. I'm taking my notebook along. Maybe he'll give me his autograph."

Ms. Benson looked at the clock in the back of the room.

"It's almost ten. Let's get in line," she told the class.

The children stood by twos in the hall.

Ms. Benson looked at Danny and said, "Let's walk quietly to the new library, and when we're there, please, make me proud of our class."

"I will," Danny said.

Beth was next to Danny in line.

"And don't tell any of your riddles," Beth said.

"Not even this one? Why don't ducks tell jokes when they're flying in the air?"

"No!"

The library was at the far end of the front hall, just beyond the gym. The children quietly followed Ms. Benson.

Danny whispered to Beth, "Don't you want to know about the ducks?"

"No!"

The four police officers whom the children had seen arrive on motorcycles were now standing in the hall near the entrance to the library. Their hands were on their hips, and they watched as Ms. Benson's class walked past.

"They would quack up," Danny whispered. "That's why flying ducks don't tell jokes."

"And it's not funny," Beth told him.

The children entered the library. Several rows of chairs were set up in the center of the room. In the back were several reporters and photographers. In front was a large desk and a microphone. Behind the desk was the librarian's office.

Ms. Benson and her class sat in the first few rows of seats. Ms. Benson sat on an end seat. Next were Danny, Beth, Cam, and Eric.

Eric turned and looked all around. Then he bent his head back and looked up.

"Wow!" he whispered to Cam. "There are windows in the ceiling."

"Those are called skylights," Cam said.

Two Secret Service agents stood by the

front desk. They watched the teachers and children enter the library.

"They give me the jitters," Danny said to Ms. Benson.

"Shh."

When everyone was seated, Dr. Prell, the principal, stepped up to the microphone.

"This is a great day for our school," she said. "We have a beautiful new library. We have Governor Zellner here. The Pearls are also here. This library is their generous gift to our school."

The library office door opened. Two Secret Service agents came out, followed by Governor Zellner and the Pearls. The governor wore a large red, white, and blue "Zellner for President" button on his jacket. Mrs. Pearl had long, curly white hair and wore a red dress and a large dangling pearl necklace. Mr. Pearl was dressed in a white suit, white shirt and tie, and white shoes.

When they walked out, lightbulbs flashed as news photographers took their pictures.

"It's my great honor," Dr. Prell announced, "to introduce our beloved governor, Elliot Zellner."

Governor Zellner stood by the microphone. He raised his hands and waved. "Thank you. Thank you," he said.

Bang!

Governor Zellner dropped to the floor.

CHAPTER TWO

The children and teachers in the room were scared. They dropped to the floor. Many of the adults standing by the sides of the room did, too. The four police officers hurried in.

Two Secret Service agents and the police officers walked slowly through the room. Cam looked behind her. All she saw were people on the floor. She turned and looked up at the large front desk.

Two Secret Service agents were crouched on the floor beside Governor Zellner. Another had pushed the Pearls behind the desk.

Cam turned and watched the two agents

and the police officers go to the back of the library. She looked at the large windows in the new library. She looked up at the skylights. She took a deep breath and then whispered to Eric, "I don't see or smell smoke. If a gun was shot in here, there would be smoke."

"Maybe someone shot from outside."

"No," Cam whispered. "The windows are closed, and not one is broken."

"Then why are we on the floor?" Eric asked. "Why do the Secret Service people look so worried?"

"They want to know what made that noise."

"I do, too," Eric said.

People in the room began to whisper.

One of the agents in the back of the room waved. Then one by the desk said, "There's no need to be afraid. Please, return to your seats."

Cam, Eric, and the others in their class looked at Ms. Benson. She looked to the back and saw the two agents who had searched the room. They were smiling. Ms. Benson returned to her seat. Then Cam, Eric, and the others did, too.

"I wonder what made that noise," Ms. Benson said.

"It wasn't me," Danny told her. "I've been good."

The two agents who had searched the room were now by the front desk. They spoke for a moment with the other two agents and Dr. Prell.

Dr. Prell laughed. She said something to Governor Zellner. He laughed, too. Dr. Prell took a large yellow book from a shelf on the side of the room. Then she tapped on the microphone to get everyone's attention.

She smiled and said, "That was frightening, but no one was hurt. This is a library. There are lots of books here, and one of them fell. We don't have carpeting yet, so when the book hit the concrete floor it made that scary sound."

Dr. Prell dropped the yellow book onto the desk.

Bang!

The book fell flat.

A few children dropped to the floor again. Others laughed.

Dr. Prell tapped on the microphone. When everyone was quiet, she introduced Governor Zellner again.

"We are delighted and proud to have him here," she said. "We hope this will be his first of many visits to our school."

The governor waved and smiled. Lights flashed as photographers took his picture.

"I am very pleased to be here," the governor said. "This is a great day for your school and our state. I am happy to share it with you and with my good friends Sam and Emma Pearl. But what's more important, the Pearls are great friends of libraries and schools."

"Please," Cam whispered to Eric, "let me have your notebook."

Eric gave Cam the notebook. She put it on her lap and pushed it off. It dropped to the floor. First the edge of the notebook hit the floor. Then it landed on its side. It made just a small sound when it hit the floor. She picked it up, put it on her lap, and pushed it off a second and a third time. Each time, it landed on its side.

"This beautiful new library," the governor said, "made possible by the generosity of the Pearls, should be a model for libraries in schools throughout the state and nation. To be truly great, a nation needs great schools, libraries, and readers!"

He waved and smiled again. Lights flashed as photographers took his picture.

"Books don't just fall," Cam whispered, "and they don't fall flat."

Mrs. Pearl went to the microphone. She was a small woman. Dr. Prell lowered the microphone for her.

"Sam and I are happy to be here with you today," Emma Pearl said. "This is where we met. We were in the same second-grade class. We're so very glad we are able to give this great school a new library."

"And books," Sam Pearl said. "We are giving the school one thousand new books."

The governor, Dr. Prell, and the others applauded.

"Something strange is going on here," Cam told Ms. Benson. Photographers took pictures of Governor Zellner, the Pearls, and Dr. Prell.

Dr. Prell said, "Let's get some children and books in the picture."

She asked Cam, Eric, Danny, and Beth to stand beside the Pearls.

"Smile!" one photographer told the children.

"Say, 'Cheese'!" another said.

Cam, Eric, and Beth said, "Cheese."

Danny said, "Parmesan and Muenster."

Lightbulbs flashed.

"Thank you," Dr. Prell told the children.

"I have to show you something," Cam told Dr. Prell. "It's very important."

"Not now," Dr. Prell said to Cam. "You'll show me later."

"But I have to show it to you now."

Dr. Prell didn't answer Cam. Instead, she stood beside Governor Zellner and posed for another picture.

CHAPTER THREE

One of the newsmen asked Dr. Prell if she remembered when the Pearls were second-graders.

"Of course not," Dr. Prell said. "That was more than fifty years ago! I haven't been principal here that long. I'm not even that old."

"Please," Cam said. "I need to show you something."

Another newsman asked the principal, "What will this new library mean to your students?"

"This library is one of the most important rooms in our school. I'm glad it's big and beautiful and filled with books."

The reporters thanked Dr. Prell. They turned and spoke with Governor Zellner.

Ms. Benson tugged on Cam's shirt and whispered, "Talk to Dr. Prell later."

"This can't wait," Cam said.

"I can't wait, either," Danny told Ms. Benson. "I have to go somewhere, and I have to go now. I have to go to the bathroom."

"What is it?" Ms. Benson asked Cam.

Danny was standing now, and hopping around.

"This is not a joke," he told Ms. Benson. "I *really* have to go."

"I have to show Dr. Prell something," Cam said. "It's about the loud noise."

Ms. Benson told Danny he could go. Then she whispered to Dr. Prell that Cam had something important to show her.

"Watch this," Cam told Dr. Prell. Then she pushed the large yellow book off the desk. It fell to the floor, but it didn't fall flat. First the edge of the book hit the floor. Then it landed on its side.

Dr. Prell was annoyed. She told Cam to pick up the book and get back to her seat.

Cam picked up the book and said, "Didn't you see what happened? Books don't just fall. They must be pushed. And when they do fall, they don't fall flat and don't make a loud noise."

Dr. Prell looked at Cam. Then she looked at the book. She pushed it off the desk. It didn't fall flat.

"I think you're right," she told Cam. "Come with me. We'll talk to one of the Secret Service agents."

Dr. Prell whispered to the female agent with long blonde hair. Then Cam followed Dr. Prell and the agent into the library office.

Cam told the agent what she had just told the principal. Then she took a book and pushed it off the desk, and again, it fell on its side.

"You're a smart little girl, aren't you?" the agent said, and smiled. "Of course, you're right. We know someone dropped the book to cause a disturbance. But we checked the room, and there's no one here who's a danger to Governor Zellner. We're sure it was just one of the children in the back who did it to be funny."

Cam thought of Danny.

Dr. Prell smiled and told Cam, "You see. It was just one of those little things that happen in schools."

It wasn't such a little thing, Cam thought. *The governor was scared. We all were.*

Cam reluctantly returned to her seat.

"You missed meeting the governor," Eric said. "We got in line and shook his hand. He even signed my notebook."

Eric showed her the governor's autograph.

"One day, this might be really valuable. He might be president."

Mr. Tone's class was in line now. Each child in turn shook hands with Governor

Zellner. The Pearls shook hands with the children, too.

Mr. Tone had brought along a camera. He stood nearby and took photographs of each child with the governor.

Cam told Eric what the agent had said.

"I don't think someone would do that just to be funny," Eric said. "Even Danny wouldn't do it. It's too scary with all these Secret Service people and police around."

"I think you're right," Cam said. "I think someone had a reason to drop that book. I just wish I knew what it was."

CHAPTER FOUR

Newspeople were still gathered around the governor and the Pearls. They were asking questions and taking photographs.

"Maybe one of the newsmen did it," Eric said. "Maybe he thought it would make a good story—'Governor Frightened by Loud Noise!' or 'Book Scares Governor Zellner!'"

"Maybe it was one of the photographers," Cam said. "I bet they all got lots of good pictures of the governor and the Pearls hiding behind the desk."

"What about *your* pictures?" Eric asked. "What about the ones you took with your mental camera?"

Cam closed her eyes. She said, *"Click!"* She tried to remember everything she had seen that morning.

"Smile," Mr. Tone told the child standing with the governor.

"I am smiling," Governor Zellner joked. "I always smile."

Mr. Tone pressed the button on his camera. *Click!*

Cam said, *"Click!"* too.

"What are you looking at?" Eric asked.

"There are so many pictures in my head. So much has happened today. Right now I'm looking at pictures of those long black cars, of the doors being opened. You should close your eyes, too," she told Eric. "Try to remember what you've seen."

Eric closed his eyes.

"Do you remember when we looked through the window?" Cam asked Eric. "First those four Secret Service agents got out of the car."

"Yes," Eric said. "I remember, but I can't

see it like you can. I remember we saw the governor, the Secret Service agents, and the Pearls."

"Me, too," Cam said. "Now, I'm looking at the Pearls."

Cam said, *"Click!"* again. Then she said, "Hey! That may be it."

Cam opened her eyes.

"It may be the pearls."

"What did they do?" Eric asked. "They didn't drop the book. Someone in the back of the library did."

"I've got to see Mr. and Mrs. Pearl."

Children had surrounded the front desk. The short Emma and Sam Pearl were mostly hidden behind them. Cam could see their faces, but nothing more.

"Please," Mr. Tone said, "squeeze closer together. I want to get everyone in the picture."

Mr. Tone was standing right behind Cam and Eric.

Cam stood. She tried to look over the heads of the children.

"You're in the way," Mr. Tone told her. "Please, sit down."

"But I must see Mrs. Pearl."

"I have to see her, too," Mr. Tone said, "and with you standing there, all I see is the back of your head."

"But this is important."

Mr. Tone was a tall man. He looked down at Cam and told her, "This picture is important to me and to every child in my class. You will just have to wait."

Cam sat. She watched and waited while

Mr. Tone told one child after another to move either to the left or to the right. He told some to crouch down a bit and others to stand taller. Then he told them to smile.

Click!

"One more," Mr. Tone said.

Click!

Mr. Tone thanked everyone. Then he told his students to return to their seats.

The children moved away from the desk. Cam stood. She looked at Mrs. Pearl.

"That's it," she said. "Now I know *why* someone dropped that book. I just have to find out *who*."

"Why?" Eric asked.

"I already told you. The pearls."

Eric looked at Mr. and Mrs. Pearl.

"They dropped the book?" Eric mumbled. "But why?"

Cam told Ms. Benson, "I have to speak with Mrs. Pearl and the Secret Service people." Then she grabbed Eric's hand and pulled him along.

The children in Ms. Kane's fourth-grade class were getting in line.

"Hello," Ms. Kane said to Governor Zellner. "It's so nice to meet you." She asked him for his signature. "I'll make copies for the children in my class."

Governor Zellner signed the paper.

Cam and Eric rushed past the governor and Ms. Kane.

"Mrs. Pearl," Cam said, "where's your pearl necklace?"

Mrs. Pearl felt for it. Then she looked down.

"My pearls! They're gone!"

CHAPTER FIVE

"My good pearl necklace is gone," Emma Pearl told her husband.

"Maybe the clasp broke," he said.

"Oh, my," Mrs. Pearl said. "I hope not. It's a gold and diamond clasp." She was very upset. "I wear that necklace everywhere."

"Don't worry," Mr. Pearl told her. "We'll find it. And if the clasp is broken, we'll get it fixed."

He told the Secret Service agent with long blonde hair about the necklace. The agent spoke into her walkie-talkie, and a police officer came in from the hall. The policeman asked the Pearls lots of questions.

"Is the necklace valuable?"

"Yes," Mr. Pearl said. "It's *very* valuable."

"Are you sure you had it on today?"

"Yes," Mrs. Pearl told the officer.

"Maybe you took it off. Maybe it fell off."

"Maybe the string broke," Sam Pearl said. "If it did, pearls are rolling all over the school."

"That's not what happened," Cam said. "Someone dropped the book to make that noise and then stole the necklace."

"That's nonsense," the agent with long blonde hair said. "Nothing was stolen. We've been with the Pearls since they came here."

The police officer said, "If the necklace was lost, we'll find it. It must be somewhere in this school."

The officer told Dr. Prell to have the children and their teachers all wait in their seats.

The Secret Service agent asked Governor Zellner and the Pearls to please wait in the library office. Two of the agents would wait with them. The other two and the police officers would look for the necklace.

Cam watched the two agents search on the floor near the desk. Then they walked slowly toward the door. They searched the floor as they walked.

Cam closed her eyes and said, *"Click!"*

The two agents left the library.

"Where are they now?" Cam asked Eric with her eyes still closed.

"They're in the hall."

"Mrs. Pearl didn't lose it in there," Cam said. "I'm looking at a picture of her when we first came into the library. She still had her necklace."

"Hi," Danny said as he sat down. "I'm back."

"You missed everything," Beth told him. "We met Governor Zellner. I shook his hand. And Mrs. Pearl lost her pearls."

"She did? How many little Pearls did she lose?" Danny asked. "And what are their names? Janie Pearl? Jackie Pearl? Jokie Pearl?"

"Stop!" Beth told him.

"I like the name Jokie."

"Well, she didn't lose her children. She lost her pearl necklace."

"Oh."

Cam opened her eyes. She got up and started toward the library office.

"Please, sit down," Ms. Benson told her.

"I can't," Cam said. "I have to speak to the Secret Service people. I know what happened to Mrs. Pearl's pearl necklace. It was stolen, and I know who did it."

CHAPTER SIX

"Are you sure?" Ms. Benson asked.

Cam nodded.

"Okay. Go ahead," Ms. Benson told her.

Ms. Benson asked Mr. Tone to watch her class. Then she followed Cam to the library office. Eric, Danny, Beth, and others in Cam's class went, too. They crowded around her as she knocked on the door.

When the door was opened, Cam said, "Someone dressed in black stole the necklace."

"Please," the agent with long blonde hair said. "Let us take care of this." She started to close the door.

Ms. Benson put her hand out and stopped the door.

"This girl is one of my best students," she told the agent. "She's very smart, and she has an amazing photographic memory. She's solved lots of mysteries. You should at least listen to her."

"Okay. I'm listening," the agent said.

"I'm listening, too," Governor Zellner said.

Cam took a deep breath.

"Someone knew that when he dropped

a book flat on a cement floor it would make a noise like a gun being shot. When Governor Zellner dropped to the floor, a man dressed in black pushed the Pearls behind the desk."

"He wanted to protect them," Governor Zellner said.

"But he wasn't one of the Secret Service people. Only four agents came with you. There was someone else dressed in black."

"Max and I were checking the governor, to be sure he wasn't hurt," the blonde agent said. "Jimmy and Susan checked the room."

"Yes," Cam said. "Those were the four agents I saw get out of those long black cars. And I saw just four when you came into the library."

"Well, someone pushed me behind the desk," Emma Pearl said. "He squeezed my arm when he pushed me."

"And he stole your necklace," Cam said.

Cam closed her eyes and said, *"Click!"*

"He has curly brown hair," Cam said, with

her eyes still closed, "round eyeglasses, and a funny little beard."

"Funny?" the agent asked. "What was funny about his beard?"

"It was crooked," Cam said. "He had on a black shirt and pants and white sneakers."

"Our shoes are black," the agent said, and held up her foot.

"Hey! I saw him," Danny said.

Cam opened her eyes.

"I was at the water fountain when that man and a real thin woman walked by. They were about to go out the back door when Mrs. Adams stopped them."

"Who is Mrs. Adams?" the agent asked.

Dr. Prell said, "She's the custodian."

"Well," Danny went on, "she pointed to a car and asked, 'Is that yours?' When the man said it was, Mrs. Adams told them not to park there again. Their car was blocking the back door."

"Don't worry," Governor Zellner told Mrs. Pearl. "We'll get your necklace back."

He hurried out of the library. The two Secret Service agents followed him. They were soon back with two police officers.

"Please," Governor Zellner said to Cam and Danny, "tell officers Taylor and Gold what you told us."

They stood just outside the library office. Cam and Danny told the officers about the thief dressed in black and the thin woman.

Officer Gold wrote what they said in a small notepad.

"I bet it was that thin woman who dropped the book," Cam said.

Officer Taylor said, "First we'll speak to Mrs. Adams. Maybe she can describe their car."

Officer Gold closed his notepad. Then he and Officer Taylor started out of the library.

"We'll go with you," Cam said. "We can help you catch the thieves."

"Yes, we'll go with you," Danny said.

"Oh, no you won't," Dr. Prell told them. "The police and the Secret Service will handle this."

Dr. Prell stepped up to the microphone. She thanked Governor Zellner and the Pearls. Then she told the teachers to take their children back to their classrooms.

Ms. Benson thanked Mr. Tone for watching her class. Then she led her children into the hall.

"Hey!" Eric said. He bent and picked up

something small, brown, and hairy from the floor. He held it by just one hair and said, "I think I've seen this somewhere."

"We've all seen it," Cam said. "We have to show it to Officers Taylor and Gold. It may help them find the thieves."

CHAPTER SEVEN

Eric showed the brown, hairy thing to Ms. Benson.

"What is it?" she asked.

Cam held it under her chin.

"It's a fake beard," Cam said. "The thief put it on to fool us."

Eric said, "We have to show it to those police officers."

Ms. Benson shook her head and said, "I'm sorry. This is not a day for you to be wandering in the halls looking for the police."

"They may not even be here," Beth said. "They may be on their motorcycles chasing the thief."

"I'll call the office," Ms. Benson said. "I'll tell Mrs. Wayne about the beard. She'll find the police."

When they returned to their classroom, Cam and Eric looked out the window. The long black cars were still in front of the school. The news truck was there, too. But two of the police motorcycles were gone.

"Tell me if you see anything," Cam said to Danny.

"I see you," Danny said. "I see Eric and Beth and Jane and Aaron."

"Stop it!" Cam said. "I agree with Beth. You're not funny. Please, just tell me if you see anything happen outside."

Ms. Benson called the school office. Then she taught a lesson on personal pronouns.

"I'm having trouble listening," Cam whispered to Eric. "I keep thinking about the necklace."

"Me, too," Eric said.

Cam looked over at Danny. He shook his head. Nothing had happened outside.

"Danny," Ms. Benson said. "What's a personal pronoun?"

"Me?" Danny asked.

"Very good."

"Hey," Danny whispered to Beth. "What did I say?"

"*Me* is a personal pronoun."

Danny smiled.

"Jane, please give me other examples of personal pronouns."

"He, she, we, and I," Jane said.

Ms. Benson talked on and on about personal pronouns. She gave examples of how they can be used in sentences. Then she told the class to open their grammar workbooks.

"Please, do the problems on page ninety-two."

Cam opened her workbook. She tried to do the work. But she kept thinking about the necklace.

"Hey! Look!" Danny said. "The motorcycles are back."

Cam, Eric, and others in the class rushed to the windows. Ms. Benson went, too. The motorcycles stopped. Two police officers got off the motorcycles.

"Look," Beth said. "It's Officers Taylor and Gold. I bet they caught the thief."

"If they did," Eric said, "it's because of Cam. She solved the mystery of the noise. She knew what was stolen."

Beth said, "I wonder why they came back."

"We just have to wait," Ms. Benson said. "I'm sure Dr. Prell will tell us what happened."

"When?" Eric asked.

"Later," Ms. Benson said. "After the governor and the Pearls leave."

The children returned to their seats.

Ms. Benson told the class, "I'm sure you're all too excited to listen to a geography lesson. So we'll have our silent reading time now."

Cam took a book from her desk. It was a mystery. She opened it. But instead of reading, she thought about everything that had happened that morning. She hoped Mrs. Pearl would get her necklace back.

Ring! Ring!

Ms. Benson lifted the telephone handset.

"Hello. . . . Yes. . . . Oh, yes."

She put the handset down.

"Dr. Prell, Governor Zellner, the Pearls, the Secret Service agents, and the police are all coming to our room." Then she looked straight at Danny and said, "I expect everyone to be on his best behavior."

"I will," Danny promised.

Eric said, "We all will."

CHAPTER EIGHT

"Straighten your desks, please," Ms. Benson said to the class.

She looked around the room.

"Oh, my," she said. She hurried to the side of the room and closed the closet doors. She saw a mess of papers on her desk. She quickly pushed them all into the middle drawer. She straightened the window shade beside her desk.

There was a knock on the door.

Ms. Benson took one last look at the room. Then she walked over and opened the door.

The bald Secret Service agent and the one

with short dark hair and a mustache walked in. They looked at the children. One opened and closed the closet doors as he walked to the back of the room. The other walked along the chalkboard toward the windows. He looked under Ms. Benson's desk. Then he walked to the back of the room, too.

Next, the two female Secret Service agents came in with Governor Zellner. Then Dr. Prell, the Pearls, Mrs. Adams, Officers Taylor and Gold, and some newspeople walked in.

"Look at Mrs. Pearl," Cam whispered to Eric. "She's wearing the necklace."

"We all came here," Governor Zellner said, "to thank the girl and boy who helped the police catch the two thieves."

Mrs. Pearl smiled. "I have my necklace."

One of the newsmen called out, "Let's get a picture of you with the two children."

Dr. Prell asked Cam and Eric to stand between the governor and Mrs. Pearl.

"He's not the boy," Officer Taylor said. "It was that one."

He pointed to Danny.

"Me?" he asked.

"Yes," Officer Gold said. "You told us that Mrs. Adams stopped them, that she told them to move their car."

Lights flashed as newspeople took lots of pictures of Cam and Danny with Mrs. Pearl and her necklace. They also took pictures of them with the governor and the two police officers.

"Tell us what happened!" one of the newsmen said.

Officer Gold told the reporters about the

dropped book and the fake Secret Service agent.

"The thief pushed me and Sam behind the desk," Mrs. Pearl said. "We thought he was one of the Secret Service people."

"He wasn't," the blonde agent said. "We're here to watch Governor Zellner. We didn't see what was happening with the Pearls."

"He pushed us and said, 'Keep down!'" Mrs. Pearl said. "I think that's when he pulled off my necklace."

"This girl described the thief to us," Officer Gold said of Cam. "And this boy sent us to Mrs. Adams."

"Their car was blocking the back door," Mrs. Adams said, "and I was expecting a delivery. I thought it was a teacher's car, so I wrote the license-plate number down. I was checking the list I have of teachers' license numbers to see whose car it was. That's when those two came by."

"And that's how we caught them," Officer Taylor said. "We had the plate number, so it

was easy. Another police officer spotted the car. There was a short chase and we caught them."

"What a great story!" one of the newsmen said. "It has everything. It has a famous man."

Governor Zellner smiled when he heard that.

"It has lots of children, a generous couple, a car chase, and a happy ending."

"This story is not done," Governor Zellner told the newspeople. "I hope Dr. Prell, Ms. Benson, and Mrs. Adams will bring this class to the state capital. I'll show them the state assembly and senate. Then they'll come to my office where we'll honor these two brave children and Mrs. Adams."

"Me?" Danny asked again.

"Yes," Governor Zellner said. "You're heroes."

"I'd like a picture of the three heroes, please," one of the photographers said.

Cam, Danny, and Mrs. Adams stood together.

Several photographers crowded around them. The newspeople stood right behind them.

Cam, Danny, and Mrs. Adams smiled. The photographer pressed the shutter button.

Click!

Cam looked at the many photographers and newspeople. She blinked her eyes and said, *"Click!"* too.

She wanted to remember this day for a long time.

A Cam Jansen Memory Game

Take another look at the picture opposite page 1. Study it. Blink your eyes and say, *"Click!"* Then turn back to this page and answer these questions. Please, first study the picture, *then* look at the questions.

1. Is Cam sitting or standing?
2. Is Cam taking a book from the book-case, or is Eric?
3. How many children are in the picture?
4. Is there a motorcycle outside?
5. What are the letters on the news truck?
6. Does Danny's shirt have stripes or dots, short sleeves or long sleeves?

F ADL
Cam Jansen and the secret service mystery

30051000000271

F
ADL   Adler, David A.

Jansen and

DUE DATE

PZ7.A2615Caqkh 2006

1.Schools—Fic
ries. I.Natti, S
III.Series: Adler
adventure ; 26.

1.Schools—Fic
tion. 3.Myste

F
ADL

Adler, David A
the secret
c2006.

LIBRARY
School No. 51